Copyright ©

Matt S

ISBN: 978-1-387-77256-8

The characters in this book are purely fictitious.

Any likeness to persons living or dead is purely coincidental.

www.mattshawpublications.co.uk

With thanks to the following supporters of my work:

Steven Wexler, Gary Harper, Bernard Galpin, Amelia Sutherland, Karen Thomas, Jessica Shelly, Steve Chappo, James Herrington, Jean Kelly, Renee Luczynski, Cat Goy, Sharen Womack, Cipher66, Jennifer Brooks, Adam Searle, Mary Kiefel, Lucy Desbrow, Jill Rogers, Jacquetta B, Sophie Harris, Kristy Lytle, Melissa Potter, Jacqui Saunders, Nigel Parkin, Amber Chesterton, Billy Smith, Chris Peart, Jon Vangdal Aamaas, Peter Le Morvan, Gemma De-Lucchi, Julie Shaw, Marie Shaw, John Burley, George Daniel Lea, Donna Cleary, Lex Jones, Joanna Taylor, Karla Rice, Scott Tootle, Louise Turner, Kevin Doe, Andiboo, Sue Newhouse, Karen McMahon, Joy

Boysen, Mason Sabre, Anna Garcia-Centner, Angela McBride, Debbie Dale, Kelly Rickard Jennifer Eversole, Cece Romano, Jennifer Burg Palfrey, Michele Fleming, Jessica Richardson

A massive, massive thank you for supporting my work and being a part of my Patreon page!

Want your name listed here?
www.patreon.com/themattshaw

SHE'LL NEVER KNOW

MATT SHAW

#1

Meet The Lonely Virgin.

According to *The Penguin Atlas of Human Sexual Behaviour* "sex" occurs 120 million times a day. 240 million people have sex daily. That's about 10 million people per hour or 166,666 people a minute. This particular title was published in the year 2000 though and since then, the world population has increased from where it was back then - a staggering figure of just under 6.1 billion people. So, with that in mind, the numbers quoted above are wrong. In actual fact, now, they will be higher and, when you read this short tale, they could be even higher still. Regardless of how accurate the figures are (or are not), though, one thing is *known* for sure; Robert Nash was *not* having sex and had *never* had sex. Not with another person anyway. There had been many an occasion he had taken matters into his own hand to find that beautiful release offered by a heavenly orgasm.

Robert was not an ugly man. He wasn't exactly a great looking guy either, though. He was just... Well. He was Robert. Just shy of six foot, a healthy looking twelve stone in weight, a good head of dark hair and kind eyes that changed colour from green to blue depending on the light they were lit with. With a little effort, and a better dress sense, he could have quite easily picked up some local tart at closing time down the local pub. Sure it wouldn't have led to a long romance or wedding bells but he could have at least scored a sloppy blow job behind the dumpster cans out back. Maybe, if she'd been plied with another tequila, the chance to finger the girl too.

'Just don't get it in my hair,' the girl would say with a lustful sigh in her voice as she jerked her hand back and forth with steady pace, desperate to get Robert's protein splashed onto her greasy complexion. And, with that, Robert would shut his eyes and clench his fists together as he felt the old welcome build-up of a leg trembling orgasm: two thoughts in his mind as his cock throbbed and spat out a thick stream of heavy gunk. 1) This felt fucking amazing. 2) If she swallows, is it classed as cannibalism?

In fairness to Robert, it wasn't effort or clothes that would have helped him score with a cheap, drunk tart. He went to the pub every Friday with his limited friends and he always dressed to impress with a nice shirt (colours vary on a weekly basis) and a good pair of slacks that fitted without the need for a belt. Going to the pub took effort - which he freely gave - and the clothes were similar to what his friends wore and they never seemed to struggle with the women. Hell, a few of them were even married and - of those few - a couple of them still managed to get attention from other women. What was stopping Robert, therefore, was not the effort or the dress sense but, instead, it was his confidence. Or should that read, *lack* of confidence. If a girl smiled at him, his face reddened and he made a hasty retreat. If a girl spoke to him, even to ask him the time so as not to miss her chance of *last orders* at the bar, and he were unable to get to an exit point - he'd stutter and stumble over his words and have to remain seated for the next ten minutes or so until his surprise erection subsided. The obvious embarrassment and frequency of unwanted erections was not something that didn't go unnoticed by his friends who loved the opportunity to tease him further.

'I'd say it was Rob's round but I think he's still trying to hide that boner from where that girl sneezed on him this morning,' one friend once joked.

'Fuck you,' Robert would reply - perfectly at ease with chatting back to his male friends. The strange thing was, Robert wasn't shy at all whilst talking to his male friends. If a human had a penis, he felt at ease chatting with them - so long as someone else made the first introductions. He didn't like making the first move. If, however, the human had a vagina, he was fucked. Metaphorically speaking.

#2
Standard Friday Banter.

'Oh fuck off and change the record.' Robert moaned to his friends as he sipped another mouthful of his first (and only) pint of lager for the evening. It was the third Friday of the month and, according to the group's self- imposed roster, it was his turn to be designated driver.

It was nine o'clock and his "friends" were already teasing him about his lack of sexual contact with another person. Some of them were asking if he was secretly gay and just too afraid to set foot out of his comfortable - and safe - closet and others were offering girls up on a plate for him; girls they knew around town who were both pig ugly and most likely to say "yes" thanks to a love of cock and a lack of willing male partners offering *it up*, so to speak.

'Heidi is a lovely girl,' Jason laughed. Heidi was far from being a lovely girl. She had a filthy mouth on her, what with her favourite word being "cunt", and she must have weighed the same as a small rhino with a stink similar to one too. A stink, the friends mused, which seeped from what they presumed to be an overly large gash that willingly yawned wider whenever an erection nearby was waiting to be swallowed whole. 'I'm pretty sure once we explain the situation to her, she'll be more than willing to take you under her bingo wings.'

'Seriously - fuck off.'

'We can tell her you're a fucking mute, or something. That way you can't scare her off with your inability to talk proper English to members of the opposite sex.' Jason suddenly remembered something funny and laughed before reminding the rest of the group, 'Hey, you all recall that time a girl asked him his name and he choked on his drink? Fucking sprayed that bitch good and proper.'

"That bitch"? How did you ever get a woman to sleep with you? Such a charmer!'

'Who wouldn't want a piece of this?' Jason got up from behind the pub table and pointed at his own body. He was an arrogant prick, yes, but credit where it was due - he had a good look about him: chiseled features, a torso which resembled an upside-down triangle thanks to the muscles beneath his tight shirt. As for his poor attitude towards the ladies - well, they seem to like a bad boy. Lots of women go for that, much to Robert's frustration - what with him regarding himself as one of the good guys. You treat them well, they run off with a bit of rough. You act like a fucking shit and they stick to you like happy, buzzing flies ready to lick you right up.

'Maybe that is your problem?' Scott joined in the conversation. One of the married men. Scott was looking directly at Robert. 'Maybe you're too damn fussy? You should just fuck Heidi and lose that V-sign hanging directly over your head. Start low, get confident and move up the ladder... I've had some dogs in my time...'

'Had some? You fucking married one!' James laughed.

'Cunt!' Scott spat back.

'How would making love to Heidi build confidence?' Robert asked.

'Making love? What are you - in the fifth fucking grade? It's "fucking". You want to *fuck* Heidi...'

'No, really, I don't...' Robert continued his original point, 'Besides - how would that build confidence? She's so fucking fat I probably wouldn't even touch the sides.'

'Like throwing a penny into a tunnel...'

'Or a pencil in a bucket.'

'Just make sure you strap a plank of wood to your arse so you don't fall in.'

'Slap that arse and ride the waves.'

'Safety rope and scaffolding for when you climb aboard.'

'A harpoon if she gets out of hand.'

'And you've proven my point. She'd laugh me out of bed.' Robert finished what he was saying.

'If you even managed to find her cunt in the first place. I know this one guy who went with a fat chick and fucked a fold of flab,' Scott said. 'He thought he was doing a good job because she was so wet for it but - yeah - it was actually sweat.'

'Mate, seriously, you need to stop talking so badly about your wife...' James ribbed him again.

'You're a fucking dick.'

Jason turned the conversation back to Heidi, 'So what do you say? Want me to hook you up?'

'No. Really. I don't.'

'Just book a hooker if it bothers you that much.' James stopped ripping the piss out of Scott's wife long enough to offer his worldly advice to Robert, who continued to squirm under the abuse he was getting from his friends. He hadn't even been the one to bring the subject of girls up. It was never him, always them. They'd start by asking if he had met anyone and, when he said no, they would start ripping into him mercilessly like a pack of hounds on an illegal hunt toying with the fox before ripping it to shreds.

'Please, I'm not *that* desperate.' Robert was lying. He had been that desperate on more than one occasion and - on more than one occasion - he had failed to go through with the appointment. Nine times out of ten (a saying, he hadn't actually tried ten times) he would hang up as soon as the working girl answered her phone. The one time he did actually book to go to the lady's house, he got to the door and then - like a frightened school boy - just kept on walking. That particular ill-fated attempt at booking such a lady being his last try at it.

'What you talking about? The way you're going, you're likely to be the only forty-year old virgin. Steve Carrel will make a shit movie about you.'

'I wonder who would play my part,' James mused.

Scott took revenge, 'Some fat, unfunny cunt.'

'Seth Rogen for sure.' Jason helped Scott finish the insult.

James shrugged and said, 'Your wife finds me funny.' Without realising, he had lined Scott up with another cheap shot.

'Only when you pull your pants down.'

James was beaten. He replied with the unoriginal middle finger raising up.'

Robert found himself relaxing a little. The more his friends turned on each other, the more they left him alone. He had had his mocking for the night, it had more or less been relentless since they'd arrived at the public house a little under two hours ago. Robert took another sip of his own beer and let them carry on attacking each other. He knew better than to join in, although the temptation was there. The moment he opened his mouth, the attention would turn back to him. That was the way it had always gone since they had first started coming down here. With the friends playfully attacking each other, he was nothing more than a willing - thankful - spectator. Unluckily for him, though, they soon grew tired. After all, to them the game was much more entertaining when the victim wasn't as quick-witted at answering back to the flying insults.

'Maybe Tom will let you fuck one of his *friends*?' Jason turned back to Robert who sighed heavily. He hadn't even been given a five minute reprieve from the verbal onslaught. He also knew exactly what Jason was referring to with the way he said "friends".

'Don't bring me into this!' Tom warned them from across the table. He had been sitting there, quietly minding his own business whilst flicking through Facebook on his mobile phone as was often the way when the group got together: something he was often teased about when they'd point out he would have been better off staying at home if he was just going to sit on *that fucking phone* all night. He would often reply with, 'Yes but the wife is home'.

Another one of the married friends although he was edging ever closer to a messy divorce.

Tom worked in the morgue at Southampton Hospital and was often ribbed for only taking on the job in order to fuck about with dead folk both in a comical way and - of course, what with lads being lads - sexual way. Never mind the fact he had gone to university and studied anatomy for years beforehand. Now his days were spent booking in the dead and doing the odd post mortem to try and find the cause of death - a task which was sometimes easy and, at other times, a complete mystery.

'Tom, mate, divorces are expensive and we all know you don't get the best wage. Think of the extra income you could get if you open the doors to sad bastards like Robert here. They pay you a fee, they come in, you step outside and keep a look out and they have their fill of dead snatch. Who knows, sometimes they might still be warm by the time they get to you. You could charge extra.' Jason laughed. Tom just looked at him as though he were mental. In some ways, he was - more so when, like now, he had had a few bevvies. Tom also gave him a look which said "shut the fuck up". The marriage problems were common knowledge but that didn't meant Tom wanted to discuss them, especially not around the pub table whilst his friends were getting more and more pissed by the minute. Jason, unsurprisingly given the way he was putting the alcohol away, didn't take stock of the look. 'And, Rob, it would be better than a hooker too. Some of those whores charge for this and that and then more for the other, and then - sometimes - you even get there only to find that what you want is off the menu anyway. Like anal, for example... It states she takes it in the shitter on her website but when you get round there she makes some cock and bull excuse about you being too big for her to accommodate. Truth was, she never allowed it anyway - just said it to get you through the fucking door. Doing one of Tom's friends - he can charge a one off fee and you can do whatever the fuck it is you want to do. Want to cream-pie arse or cunt? Sure. Want to knock one off over tits, face or - fuck it - feet? Up to you. Your money, your time and the dead don't complain...'

Robert was uncomfortable with this conversation. Not because he was offended with thoughts of sticking a cock into a dead person but because he knew Tom was in a mood. He had been quiet before but tonight, he seemed even more so. Quietly seething, ignoring the banter of friends and seemingly scrolling the same pages on Facebook over and over whilst constantly refreshing his messages as though waiting for something, or rather *someone*. He tried to turn the line of conversation back to everyone attacking Jason again by saying, 'Sounds like he has given this too much thought, right? Tom - Jase ever ask you if he can fuck a corpse?'

Tom slid his mobile back into his pocket and turned to Robert with a serious look on his face. He said, 'I've got to get up early in the morning. Work. You cool to drop me off home now?' Tom's request came as a surprise to most people sitting at the table. If he went home now, it would be the first time in as long as any of them could remember that they hadn't all stayed until last orders were called.

'Sure.' Robert nodded. He was unsure whether Tom really did have work in the morning or whether he had just had enough with Jason for this evening. If it was the latter, he couldn't blame him. Jason did get overbearing when the alcohol took a hold and - today it had taken a hold faster than usual, no doubt due to the fact he had confessed to not eating anything for lunch as he had run out of time. Drinking on an empty stomach was never a good idea.

As Tom stood and took his coat from the back of his chair, the others protested his early departure by begging him to stay for one more but Tom was adamant he wanted to leave now. Work was, after all, important to him. He had trained hard for the job and he took it seriously despite their teasing. Rightly so too, when you're dealing with the dead. Robert didn't ask him to stay for another beer. He was happy to take him home as it meant he got a bit of a break from the piss-taking. He just told the others that he would be back as soon as he had dropped Tom home. The journey wasn't exactly taxing; Tom lived about fifteen minutes away if that. The whole journey there and back would most likely take less than thirty minutes if Robert put his foot down, not that he planned to. He was looking forward to a little peace and - truth be told - conversation with someone who wasn't completely steaming drunk. He figured it would be good for Tom too. Clearly he had something on his mind that he would benefit from sharing with an impartial ear. Unlike the others, when Robert was told something in confidence it stayed that way - no matter how much drink he had, a little fact the rest of the group knew too.

'Thanks for this,' Tom said as they left the group, walking towards the exit.

Robert held the door open for Tom. 'My pleasure.'

#3
Women Troubles.

Robert asked Tom if everything was okay the moment they got out of the pub and away from their inebriated friends. Tom nodded and said everything was fine but Robert knew there was something on his mind due to the way he said it. His tone was different and he wouldn't look him in the eye when he spoke. Instead he stared into the distance as though keeping a look out for a change of luck on the horizon, like maybe a pot of gold at the end of the rainbow. Robert didn't push him for the truth. If he wanted to talk, he would talk in his own time. Pushing him into it would only serve to piss him off and drive him further away. The drive home was quiet with only the radio presenter and hum of the car's engine stopping it from being completely silent. Another tell-tale sign that something was clearly on Tom's mind. Usually he would at least pass the time with conversation, never of anything in particular - just idle chit chat. After the abuse he had suffered in the pub, though, Robert didn't mind the lack of communication between the two of them. He simply sat there, eyes fixed on road, and enjoyed listening to the radio guy presenting the various Friday evening dance tracks. Robert knew he'd yearn for this quiet time the moment he got back to the pub when, no doubt, the others would have moved from beers to shots. God he hated being designated driver. At least when he got to drink too, the "jokes" didn't seem to bother him as much. It was always the same when he was the sober one, though. The jokes always seemed to cut that little bit deeper and he'd disappear home, after dropping them off to their own homes, and wonder what the hell was wrong with him. Was he really that much of a loser he couldn't get a girlfriend, or even a fuck?

Was he a closet homosexual who was so far in denial that his own brain had yet to admit it to himself? Did he even want anything more than a quick fumble with someone anyway? Tom had a wife, he was miserable. Scott had a wife and yet still approached other women, often fucking them when the opportunity arose. Going from his friends, having a partner didn't automatically make you a happier person and sleeping around with loads of women... Well... Robert laughed to himself when he remembered Jason describing his experiences down the sexual health clinic when one girl gave him an infection.

'They stuck a fucking swab inside of my cock. I shit you not, they opened up the jap-eye and just stuck this cotton bud down the length of my shaft. Next time I'll just live with the infection. Fuck the oozing puss...

Nothing is worth having someone stick something inside of your cock. Isn't natural.' Jason had been drunk before he openly admitted this to the group of friends.

To this day, they still occasionally brought it up in order to embarrass him a little further but only really when he was chatting up another girl; they would call out from the other side of the room and ask him if his penis had stop ejaculating yellow puss yet. Needless to say, the girls he was chatting to would often lose interest and walk away with a grimace on their face and Jason would return to the group minus the woman's phone number. Good, old friends.

'What's funny?' Tom noticed Robert laugh to himself.

'Just remembered that time Jason had to go to the clinic. Don't know why, just popped in my head.'

Tom smiled but didn't laugh. Even the thought of his embarrassed friend going through various unpleasant medical examinations wasn't enough to pull him from the slump and for good reason too. He knew that, on Monday, he would be going through the same treatment himself. 'Keep a secret?' he asked Robert.

'Sure.'

'I have to have the same tests on Monday.'

Robert shot him a look, a quick glance to try and determine whether his friend was telling him the truth or not. He was married and - unlike the others - as far as Robert was aware, he hadn't been seeing anyone else. When the group went out on the piss, no matter what state Tom got into (and he had been in some pretty messy states), never once did Robert see him even looking at another woman, let alone talking to one long enough to exchange numbers or set up a quick fuck in one of the toilet cubicles. Tom noticed the quizzical look and explained, 'She fucking cheated on me.'

'What?' Robert had heard what Tom said. He just didn't believe it. He knew they had problems and were looking to split from each other but he didn't know there was another man involved in the messy break-up. 'I'm sorry, man.' Robert said before Tom felt the need to repeat himself. Another thing which put Robert off from relationships, the way couples could hurt each other like this. Cheating was a messy business and he often thought poorly of his friends who found it so easy to cop off with someone else when they had a wife waiting at home, or even a "steady" girlfriend back home. He believed that, if you weren't happy, you should deal with the problems at home first. Let the partner know that you no longer wish to be with them, or exclusive to them at least, and then they have the chance to meet someone else too.

'Some prick from work. Thing is, that prick from work was also seeing other people and she ended up getting crabs. Fucking crabs, man. I thought that was something only teenagers got at school discos. What kind of man, in his thirties, manages to catch crabs?'

'I don't think they care how old a person is, to be fair.'

'I mean, it serves the bitch right. I'm glad she got them but... The other day, both drunk, we ended up doing what married couples do. Or rather, what they're supposed to do and - yep - I catch them too.

Now I need to go to the fucking clinic to get a complete going over to make sure the prick didn't pass anything else on that might not be quite as visible. Anyway it's just another nail in our already well-nailed coffin. Part of me hopes he had AIDS and passed that shit over to her too.'

'Wow. That's harsh.'

'Fuck her.'

'Not if she has AIDS.' Robert smiled at Tom but got nothing back. Tom was clearly angry and - to be fair - he had every right to be. It was bad enough his wife was sleeping around but to catch an infection and pass it on to Tom too? It couldn't really get any worse than that. 'Anyway, I won't tell the others. To be honest, I thought there must have been something wrong, you've been pretty quiet all night.'

'Well it's not just that. There's money issues too.' Tom admitted. Robert didn't pry. "Money issues" was pretty self-explanatory. Regardless of the fact he hadn't questioned him, Tom continued, 'Divorces aren't cheap. Should have signed a fucking prenuptial agreement. Hindsight, hey, a wonderful thing.' Robert stayed quiet still. He didn't feel the need to mention the fact that, in hindsight, Tom would have been better off not proposing to Sally in the first place. Everyone said it was too soon though. They had dated for three months before she moved in and then, more or less straight away, they were engaged. It all happened so fast that people actually thought there could well have been an ulterior motive, like an unexpected pregnancy. Given the circumstances, luckily that was not the case. There were no children involved.

'Sounds like you're really going through a bad time of it.'

'I tell you, it fucking sucks at the moment.' Tom laughed for the first time that evening, 'Things are so shitty that when Jase made that suggestion, about hiring out the corpses to people who like that kind of thing, I actually thought it made sense. I mean, sure people would want that, right? People have fetishes for everything these days - why wouldn't there be someone who likes dead people too? And, again he is right, the dead won't complain that they don't get an orgasm too if you shoot too early, they won't say no, they won't cry rape...' He stopped. Robert was just looking at him with one eyebrow raised. 'What?'

'Sounds like you want to have a go yourself.' He laughed and shook his head.

Tom shrugged and said, 'I wish I did. Had I gone down that route instead of the one I chose, I wouldn't be in the situation I'm in now, would I?' Robert didn't answer as Tom made a very good point. 'Besides, they're people. They're just a little colder than the normal person.'

'And they don't move.'

'Trust me, some of the women I went with back in my college days... They didn't move either. Had to occasionally stop to check they were still breathing and that they hadn't died whilst I was pumping away,' Tom explained. Robert laughed at the thought of someone coming and going at the same time but kept the thought to himself. 'What about you?' he asked suddenly.

Robert frowned, puzzled by the question. Tom explained in more detail, 'Would you fuck a dead person? I mean, not a mangled one but a pretty one...'

Robert laughed again and had to ask, 'Is there such a thing as a pretty dead person?'

'You would be surprised. Who is your favourite model?'

'Model? Like my favourite pin-up girl?'

'Yes. Who is your favourite?'

Robert shrugged. 'Quite a few I like. Maybe Kelly Brook. No. Bianca Beauchamp, this model who dresses in latex clothes for the majority of her shoots. She has the most amazing head of red hair... Looks like fire.'

'Easy tiger. Was a simple question. I don't need a full-on report on the girl. But, okay, whatever. Imagine she had just died. Something went pop in her head and she dropped dead. Yeah?'

'What a waste.'

'She's brought down to the morgue, ready for a post mortem examination and she's still warm... She's lying there, naked, on the table. Tits out. Shaved pussy... No one is around and no one will be around. No cameras. Nothing. Just you and this naked girl you fancied when she was breathing. Knowing in mind she hasn't changed much in the twenty minutes or so since she died... She still looks like her, but a little paler, and she still smells of her perfume. Wouldn't you be tempted to just stick it in her?' Tom stopped talking and took a breath, allowing Robert the opportunity to respond. Robert didn't respond though. He just sat there, looking at his friend with his mouth slightly agape. In his mind, he was running through the possible scenario. The answer that Tom waited for, the answer that Robert was so unsure of to begin with, slowly came to mind and took him by surprise. Well, *yes*, if he could have sex with her and no one would ever find out, he probably would. After all, it can't be rape as she hasn't said "no" (although there is an argument that nor would she have said "yes") and he was pretty sure it wasn't a crime, although in a hypothetical game of "would you fuck a corpse" the question of prison or no prison wasn't really playing on his mind. He just remembered that a judge once determined a corpse could not be a victim because the corpse wasn't considered to be a person anymore. A grey area for sure.

'I guess. Maybe.' Robert shrugged. 'I don't know.' A thought popped into his head which swayed the answer to lean more towards the negative. He continued, 'No.'

'No?'

'No because someone would know.'

'No one would know.'

'If I had sex with her there would be tell-tale signs. For example, semen in the vagina.'

'But the medical practitioner carrying out the examination has been paid off. He wouldn't report the findings. He would simply get rid of any trace evidence that might be visible to the naked eye and that would be it. Like I said, no one would ever know.'

'Well then, maybe?'

'I would fucking do it,' Tom said. 'Kylie Minogue ends up on the slab, I would definitely fuck that ass. Christ, if she died in those silver little hot pants she wore in that music video I'd probably shoot my load the moment she got wheeled in.'

'Wouldn't you feel ashamed?'

'Of having sex with a person?' Tom answered. The thought of what the judge had said about a corpse not being a person once again popped into Robert's mind and he explained the point to Tom who answered, 'A corpse isn't a person? So then - what is it? An inanimate object? If that is the case, more reason to say "yes". I've lost count the number of times I've fucked inanimate objects in my time. Ever fucked a sex doll?' Robert blushed. The reddening of his face was enough of a tell-tale for Tom to guess that it was a "yes". 'Inanimate object,' Tom pointed out. 'And did you know, I can't remember the country, there was once a television program about people who fucked Pot Noodles. Fucking Pot Noodles.... Some horny fuck decided to get amorous with a pot of noodles once they had cooled sufficiently to do so. And hoovers. People do that, that's a thing.' He stopped for a moment,

'The more I think about it, the more I reckon Jase was onto something... I reckon people would queue up to fuck corpses. Just think, you get to do what you want, no shame, no embarrassment if you shoot early or can't perform, and no answering back, no nagging, no wondering if they're having a good time, just an empty cunt ready for you to fuck as you see fit.' He paused a moment and pondered out loud, 'I just wonder where you'd fucking advertise it.'

Robert steered the car left, down onto Market Street and pulled up on the left hand side of the road. Tom's house, which he still shared with Sally, was on the right but there was nowhere available to park on that side. There never was. With no off-street parking, it was always a free-for-all on the road with people looking to dump their vehicles. Robert put the car into neutral and applied the hand-brake. 'Well here we are.'

Tom ignored him and carried on trying to make the idea of fucking a dead person more acceptable to Robert. He said, 'You know what is scary?' Robert shrugged. 'This probably already happens. I bet, somewhere in the world, there is some guy offering up dead bodies for people to fuck. The world is a dark place and it is something I have seen before in films. Well, okay, in the film it wasn't a corpse being rented out to the punter...'

'It wasn't?'

Tom shook his head. 'No, it was a chick in a coma. One of the male nurses called his friends, they came in with cash in hand. The nurse went through the rules and then let them into the private room where this girl was. One by one they took it in turn to fuck her as the nurse kept watch whilst counting out the cash.' Tom paused a moment. 'I think that's wrong.'

'It is?'

'Sure. The woman is alive. She doesn't want to be fucked. She hasn't agreed to it. That's rape.'

'She hasn't agreed to being fucked when dead either.'

'Well she can't. She's dead.'

'So if she doesn't say "yes" and she doesn't say "no" then technically it is rape.'

'If she were a person. You said it yourself, the judge didn't consider the dead body as a person and so... She wasn't a victim.' Tom cut to the chase. 'What I am saying is, if you want to do it... If you want me to fix you up with a pretty looking girl the next time one comes in who is intact and still fresh... Did you want me to call you so you can fuck her before I release the body back to whoever wants it? No one would know but you and me and I wouldn't tell anyone. It would be our secret. Who knows, maybe I'll even test her out first for you? Make sure I get you a good one. And I could even warm her a little with hot water bottles, or something, so that - when you got there - she was still warm for you. What do you say?' Robert sat there in shock for a moment. Listening to Tom, you would imagine him to be steaming drunk with what was coming from his mouth but he wasn't. He had only had a couple of beers in the time his friends had gotten through more. He was still sober. Not drunk, just insane. 'Our secret,' he said again, hoping for an answer.

'No. Not for me. But thank you.' Robert didn't really know what else to say but that was the only answer he could give. The whole thing just felt *wrong*. Whether the judge thought of a dead person as a person or not didn't come into it. *He* thought of them as a person. They were someone's daughter, someone's friend, relative... Whatever. They were a person.

Tom shrugged. 'A shame,' he said, 'could have helped us both out. You could have gotten the confidence brought on from fucking to be able to approach living girls and I could have used some of the money to finish paying for this divorce. Ah well.' He smiled at his friend and said, 'Thank you for the lift anyway and - if you ever change your mind - you know where I am. Our secret.' With that he winked at him and climbed from the car, slamming the door shut behind him. Robert paused a moment and shook his head. He couldn't believe the conversation they'd just had.

'Fucking ridiculous,' he muttered to himself before selecting the first gear, releasing his hand-brake, and continuing on down the road where he could perform a U-Turn back towards the pub. *The pub?* God knows how pissed his already drunk friends were by now. Robert was just about done for the night, he could do with going straight home - not playing taxi to his friends and having to listen to more of their bullshit. He sighed. Least it is close to closing time now. Won't be long before he could go home and draw a line under what had been a long (and strange) day.

#4

A Real Doll.

Robert pulled into his drive and opened the door before turning the engine off. He climbed from the driver's seat and stood up straight on the paved drive, gagging as he leaned down to the door to do the window up. The stink of vomit from the rear of the car hit the back of his throat: a harsh acidic smell of stomach bile and cheap lager, deposited by Jason moments before he was dropped off at his own house. He slurred something which sounded like an apology before he climbed from the car and staggered towards his front door, fumbling for his door key. Robert didn't curse him despite the urge being as strong as the stink. There was little point. He knew Jason was an aggressive drunk and even though he would have been no problem to over power in his drunken state, it wasn't worth the fight. Instead, Robert considered calling on him the following day and asking for a contribution towards having the car professionally cleaned out. For now, though... Robert switched the car's engine off and pulled the keys from the ignition. He slid them into his pocket and pushed the car door shut before walking to his own front door. He was tired, he felt sick from having to drive with the scent of vomit lingering in his lungs and the last thing he wanted to do right now was have to clean up. Anyway, he figured it would be easier to do it in the morning when it was drier: a wire brush to scrape it clean when it looked more like a stain and less like the inside of someone's suffering stomach lining. He reached his front door and, realising he needed his keys once more, pulled the keys from his pocket. He slid the larger, gold, Yale key into the lock and twisted the door open. He stepped in, breathed a sigh of relief at the thought of finally being home, and then closed the door. Just him now. No more banter from his friends, which had bordered on aggressively offensive during the drive home. No more feelings of inadequacy at the teasing they had given him for not having a girlfriend. Nothing. Just him.

He walked to the living room doorway and froze, staring into the empty room, his eyes fixed on the settee in the far corner of the room. He imagined a woman - pretty - sitting there with a smile on her face, pleased to see him. On the coffee table in front of the settee he imagined a warm cup of tea and a plate of biscuits. He imagined the woman - maybe named Karen - telling him that both were for him after she had heard him arrive home He'd walk across the room, he'd slump down - tired - on the settee next to her and then lean across for a kiss. Then he'd drink the tea and eat the biscuits before she handed him the television controller. After a long day, he deserved to put his feet up and watch his favourite programs. Robert sighed. There was no tea. There was no woman. There was no plate of biscuits. The only thing possible true in the imagined scenario being the opportunity to watch whatever television channel he fancied and at this time of night, there was only one that he desired. Robert crossed the room and sat on the sofa. Reaching for the remote control, he switched the television on. An older set, the picture slowly rolled onto the screen. Five past midnight and the program had already started: *Babestation*. On screen two pretty girls gyrated on a bed in nothing but lingerie. Both of them had phones pressed to their ears and were chatting, laughing, with people who had called in. The number to call was displayed on the right of the screen, a number Robert had never once called although - in fairness - he had never been tempted. Watching this program wasn't because he wanted to call in. He had no interest in talking to the girls. He just liked to watch them gyrate there, grinding down on the bed as though they were fucking a man (or woman). Ten minutes watching them and then he'd go upstairs. Not to *his* bedroom but - instead - to *her* bedroom. Or rather, the room he had set aside for her. Ten minutes to get images of the glamour girls pretending to kiss each other and finger themselves on stuck in his mind and then a quick session with *her* to help relieve some of the pent up tension he had accumulated during the frustrating evening. As the girls played around on screen, all clearly fake for show only, Robert reached down and started to stroke himself through his slacks. He sighed as his erection started to slowly grow. His hand, he imagined, was actually one of their hands.

*

She was not cheap and neither did she look it, lying there on his spare bed dressed in the expensive lingerie he had ordered from the site where he had placed the original order for her. She was his secret, kept from his friends who would only want to see her and then mock both her and him - him especially when they'd no doubt ask her cost. No.

They didn't need to know about her. No one did. No one needed to know about the website, no one needed to know about the order and no one needed to know he'd maxed out his credit card right up to the full amount. Besides, even if they did know, they would only make him feel bad for enjoying her company and, after spending all that money, he didn't want them ruining it for him. He wanted no one to ruin it. 'Our secret,' he muttered to himself. All of a sudden, Tom's words came flooding back to him. He had spoken the exact same sentence. Robert shook the thought from his mind and stepped into the room. For what he was imagining now, he didn't want Tom in his mind. He wanted none of his friends there, only the two playful models who'd been fooling around on the television a handful of well-spent minutes earlier.

Standing opposite the bed, in the middle of the room, with his eyes fixed on her - Robert undid the top button of his slacks. He lowered them down to his ankles, along with his boxer shorts, and stepped from them until he was only wearing socks and an average erection on the bottom half of his body. He undid the top few buttons on his shirt and then pulled it over his head before letting that drop to the floor too.

'I missed you today whilst I was at work,' he said. 'You had a good day?' He walked back to the doorway and flicked the light-switch up. A bulb hanging from the centre of the ceiling illuminated the room and brought her from the darkness she had been lying in since he had last visited. He smiled when he saw her. She was in the same outfit he had put her in the last time he came to this room: black lingerie consisting of french knickers and a matching black bra. The stockings she wore on her legs were of the hold-up variety. Her hair was dishevelled from his last visit even though he had meant to come in on many an occasion since then to give it a tidy up. It was, after all, not cheap and he knew it would be bad to let it get knotted although, if it were to ruin, the website did at least offer replacements. For a cost. He took a step towards the bed and suddenly stopped a moment with his eyes still fixed upon her perfect body; a body shape he had chosen from the various options the site had presented. He could have had a thin girl, he could have had a larger girl, even an average one and yet he chose the perfect hour glass figure with a nice round arse, small waist line and ample bosom. Modelled after Bianca Beauchamp, with her red hair, she was his ideal woman and yet the conversation with Tom back in the car had ruined that for him. The conversation had made him realise she was nothing more than a toy. A very expensive sex doll that only the elite could realistically afford without putting themselves in a certain amount of debt. The illusion of seeing her as a real person, posable in any position he fancied for that particular liaison, was shattered. He was about to fuck a toy. Tom's words echoed in his head telling him that people fuck anything these days. Sure, she wasn't a hoover or a Pot Noodle and - supposedly - her vagina was as close to real as you could get but... Still a toy. Still not a real snatch. Still not the real feeling of a pussy gripping the shaft of his cock, milking it for all it had to offer. Just a toy. He sat on the edge of the bed as his cock drooped from fully erect to nothing more than a semi. Give it a couple of minutes longer and even that would be gone, leaving him with a flaccid, good for nothing prick.

Robert looked at the doll. She did look good for a toy but now the illusion was ruined and he couldn't imagine her as a real girl, he couldn't help but feel like an idiot having spent just shy of three thousand pounds on what was - in reality - nothing more than a masturbating aid. All that money and for what? She wasn't real and couldn't offer him what he was looking for in life. His face reddened as his awkward embarrassment continued to sink in. What if someone came in when he was fucking her? How pathetic would he have looked? Worse yet - what if he died suddenly at work or, maybe, crossing the road? His mum and dad would come to clear out his house and what would they find? They'd find their son's luxury fuck toy lying in bed waiting for their son's rampant attention. Looking back at the body, lying there motionless, he continued linking Tom's words to the doll. She was not real, she never would be. She was an inanimate object and - technically - that put her in the same category as a dead person, according to the judge. Neither was a person. There was one major difference between corpse and doll, though, and that was the corpse *used* to be a real person. If Robert were to fuck a dead person, what he would be fucking would not be man-made (unless she had a designer vagina but

Robert realised that just confused the issues) like this doll was. It would be a *real* vagina and - thinking along those lines - his cock slowly started to rise once more. By the time Tom's words came to mind again, 'our secret', Robert was fully erect and his heart pounding hard and fast with a newfound sense of excitement. Adrenaline flowed through his body and blood continued to harden his already impressive erection... The Real Doll might not have been real, and he may have been embarrassed at the prospect of being caught with it, but - for now - it would serve his needs. He climbed onto the bed and lay next to her. His hand stroked through her knotted hair. The only difference from this time, to the other times he had done this, was that he wouldn't talk to her as though she could hear him. Tonight, she was just a toy.

#5

Unknown Territory.

Tom woke from a dream already forgotten with a crippled back and a hangover from Hell. The backache thanks to an uncomfortable night on the living room sofa and the hangover thanks to the decision to come into the house last night and open the bottle of whiskey he'd been given from a relative last Christmas. Half a bottle in and he had passed out right where he was sitting. The glass used to deliver whiskey from bottle to mouth was on its side on the floor, the carpet around it smelling of pure alcohol. He didn't care, he picked the glass up and set it on the coffee table. No need to care about spillages anymore. Give it a month, maybe two, and he wouldn't be living here anyway thanks to the divorce. Neither of them would be as neither he nor

Sally could afford to buy the other one out. The house would be sold and whatever monies left over from the sale, if any, would be split evenly between the two of them. That was how he presumed it would go anyway but he could be wrong. The way she was talking, she wanted more than her fair share and - knowing his luck recently - the judge would most likely rule in her favour. Hell, for all he thought now, he could end up with absolutely nothing. He had heard tales of such stories: marriages collapsing and the men ending up homeless on the streets without a penny to their names whilst the women went off and re-married, living happily ever after. He belched a heavy, gassy burp from the depths of his aching gut. He gagged at the alcoholic aftertaste from the bubble of air pulled up from the depths of his stomach. Of course the worst thing about going through a divorce, whilst being hungover at least, was the lack of compassion from the other half who'd usually get up and cook him a full English in order to soak away some of the alcohol and relieve that feeling of nausea which tended to accompany the banging head. No such luck today. In fact, knowing her, she would get up and cook herself one just to eat it in front of him, despite not actually wanting it. He wouldn't put it past her.

Tom sat up. His head pounded hard. Some asshole living inside of his cranium banging on a steel drum. He closed his eyes a minute as the room spun around. Oh God, don't throw up. Not here. Only when he felt more balanced did he open his eyes, but slowly. The room still spun but not as bad this time. Okay. Move slowly. It's better if you do not make any sudden movements. Carefully, he leaned towards his phone before turning the screen towards his slightly hazy vision. Nine percent left on the battery charge and... His alarm went off. He swiped the "off" tab onscreen unable to remember why he had even set an alarm for a Saturday. He didn't have to work today and there was nothing else he had planned to do, hence his decision to open up the much needed bottle of whiskey. He belched again at the thought of the high percentage booze. God, don't think about the whiskey. Think about anything but the whiskey. Anything like... He noticed a little envelope on the screen of his phone, signifying a waiting text message. Maybe it was Sally, he thought. Maybe she had gone to bed and then worried when she woke up in the early hours and found he wasn't sleeping next to her. He laughed to himself at the thought of her suddenly caring. It was an especially stupid thought considering the last thing she had said to him, before he went to the pub with his friends, was that she wished he would end up on one of the slabs he put the dead bodies on back at work. Here was the woman who once told him that she loved him, now wishing for him to die. Charming. He had married a real lady. Of course he bit and started shouting back at her saying that, if she were to end up on his slab, it would be because he had put her there. And, continuing on from that when - really - there was no need, he described how he would fuck with the body to turn her into the monster he knew to live not far beneath the skin. He threatened to remove her skin, then threatened to cut away the dead heart (if he could find it) and throw it in the trash and... He shook his head as the conversation played back in his mind. It wasn't long before she had been on the phone to the police stating he was threatening her. A heavy sigh escaped his lips when he wondered whether he was a wanted man. No doubt they would, at the very least, want a little chat with him. Easy to sort out but, another sigh, probably at the expense of more legal fees for having his lawyer sit with him whilst he went through everything just to make sure he didn't leave himself open to a charge. That would be all he needed.

Tom clicked through to the waiting message. Part of him wondered who it was, another part of him presumed it was probably a spam text like, say, from his local pizza shop offering another deal enticing him to spend more on takeout and - finally - a little part of him didn't really give a fuck. In the messages screen there was the list of his previous messages from friends and concerned family members asking if he was okay as they hadn't heard from him for a while. At the top of the list was a new, unread message from Robert. Tom's face flushed when he recalled the conversation from last night and Robert's reaction. He probably thinks he is a right weirdo now and has no doubt told everyone else at the pub too, if only to get the conversation away from his lack of partner for the night. A little reprieve from the usual verbal onslaught of mockery he tended to face on a weekly basis. Tom clicked the message suspecting the worse and read:

So hypothetically - how much would it cost if I were to have said "yes"?

Tom frowned a moment. Was he referring to the macabre offer Tom had made in the car giving Robert the opportunity to come to his office one evening? He had to be. Tom was hungover, definitely, but he still managed to recall yesterday's conversations. He hadn't got himself so drunk that he was left with nothing but blackness when he tried to recall what he had done the previous night. And - thinking back to the conversations - he and Robert hadn't spoken about anything else that night which could have prompted such a text. Tom sat back on the settee with his aching back still screaming at him albeit a little quieter now he wasn't bent over the phone at the coffee table. He thought for a moment, wondering how best to answer. In the end he settled for an amount instead of £250 for the hour. He figured it was better than asking Robert to clarify what he meant - a text assuming the message was even meant for Tom in the first place. By answering with a figure, if the message was about something else or it was for someone else - well then, Robert would soon reply stating as such. He waited a moment with his eyes fixed on the screen. Looking at Robert's initial text it was sent about thirty minutes ago so he was definitely up. The question was, was he sitting there cradling his own phone just as Tom was doing the same this end?

A couple more moments went by and Tom was about to give up when the phone vibrated in his hand as another text came through. Robert. With a quickened heartbeat he clicked the envelope icon and opened the message. Within were two words and nothing else. They read, *Our Secret*. Tom frantically tapped out his reply, *Of course*. His phone vibrated again and, again, he promptly read the text message that came through. *Can you meet today?* Tom smiled. Not only was there the opportunity to make a little easy money for just turning a blind eye whilst at work but he also had an excuse to get out of the house and away from Sally for a couple of hours. Suddenly his hangover wasn't feeling quite as bad.

*

'What made you change your mind?' Tom asked Robert.

The pair had met up in an off-street cafe in the centre of town and had taken seats in a corner booth, away from prying eyes as though having some secret affair. When they spoke they did so in hushed tones so the wandering waitress, offering hot drinks and menus for people wanting a cooked breakfast, couldn't hear them. Although Tom was the one suffering with a banging headache, thanks to the previous night, Robert looked just as tired and under the weather as though he too were suffering an unforgiving hangover. Tom immediately regretted his question the moment he asked it. He wanted Robert to go through with this and, although he thought it to be creepy despite what he had said in the car last night, he didn't want to suddenly put him off by placing doubt in his mind that it *was* okay to do.

'That judge,' Robert said. He continued, 'He said that the dead woman was no longer a person so couldn't be classed as a victim, right?' Tom nodded but didn't say anything. 'So technically it wasn't a crime...' Again Tom nodded even though he knew that, actually, in this country it *was* a criminal offence to sleep with the dead just as it was illegal to fuck an animal. 'And she is now reduced to nothing more than an inanimate object, that's what we said.'

'We did.'

'You told me men fuck hoovers.'

'They do.'

'Along with other weird things not meant for sticking a cock in.' 'Like Pot Noodles.'

'Exactly. And I could go and do those things, like those other men...' Robert continued as Tom sat opposite wondering whether Robert had already tried to rape a hoover by sliding his cock into the nozzle and whacking up the suction as high as it would go. Tom stifled a smile not wishing to ruin Robert's explanation or, again, make him feel as though he was being weird with agreeing to this little deal of his. 'But with the dead body there is one major difference to having sex with that over, say, a hoover or even one of those plastic and silicone vagina toys you can get.'

'A flesh-light,' Tom corrected him with the vagina toys official name. He realised the correct terminology wasn't important right now and asked, 'What's the major difference?'

'The fact the dead body *used* to be a person.'

'Indeed she was.'

'So when you're having sex with it, it might be an inanimate object but the truth of the matter is, it is still a real vagina you're inside of.'

'That is it.'

'So it has to be less weird than banging away at a toy or a household appliance or...'

'A lot less weird,' Tom lied. It was safe to say Tom had never once seen a dead body get wheeled into his place of work and thought about having sexual intercourse with it. Everything he had said, the previous night, was said with the aim of raising some more money to help with his mounting debt and for no other reason. Half the time, when working on the dead, he wasn't evening thinking about the person at all. His brain would switch to autopilot as he worked and he would be thinking about other things he had to do, such as paperwork, or he would be considering what to have in the canteen for lunch. If his thoughts did switch to the dead person, they would be more along the lines of thinking what a shame it was for someone to die so young or thoughts similar. Never once had he thought about sticking his dick up inside them. Still, the money would be handy.

'So what happens now then?' Robert asked. He was both excited and embarrassed at the same time. As Tom carefully considered his answer, wondering whether to call the whole thing off, Robert reached into his pocket and removed a wad of notes. He held it up to Tom and then slid the money back into his pocket. 'That's the full amount if you want payment up front.' The sight of the money, and the prospect of getting more of the same if Robert had a good time, was enough to remove any doubt as to whether this was the right thing to do or not from Tom's mind. 'I wasn't sure if you would want payment first, or after.'

'I can take the payment now,' Tom said as he offered his hand out. Robert removed the cash from his pocket once more and handed it to Tom who quickly pocketed it before Robert could change his mind again. 'Of course I can't do refunds if you get there and suddenly change your mind,' Tom explained. 'You know, if the dead body creeps you out in some way, or if the smell puts you off...'

'The smell?'

'The dead have a kind of aroma,' Tom confessed. 'But I'll reduce the risk of that by getting you a fresh one and - worst case - I keep air freshener in one of the cupboards. You're welcome to use a squirt of that if it would help.' Tom quickly changed the subject back to Robert's question of what happens next. 'Truth be told I haven't really considered what happens next but,' he said, 'the first thing we need is a likely candidate and I can tell you this for nothing - at the moment I do not have any ready.' In the fridges back at the morgue he had one obese man who had suffered a massive heart attack, waiting collection, and he had an old woman who passed naturally. The only other person was a Jane Doe and she had been there for a good few days now and hadn't been in a good state when she was initially brought in. 'If you keep your phone on you,' Tom suggested, 'I can call you up when one comes in. You can then come on down and...'

'I might be at work.'

'You won't be. I'll be calling you on one of my night shifts,' Tom told him. 'It is quieter so less chance of someone disturbing you. You see, I have this worked out. You will go in with the body, right, and I will wait outside the room with my phone in my hand. If someone comes down the hallway I'll quickly press your number on my phone, calling you. You stop what you're doing, get off and cover her up - and yourself. Then, you pretend to grieve for the dead body. I'll just say you're a relative.' Robert didn't say anything. He was just sitting there, nodding along quietly. Tom's plan did sound as though it had little room for error or little risk of being caught.

'How long do you think I will have to wait?' Robert asked.

Tom shrugged. 'Depends when they die. That I don't get a say in but, if it makes you feel better, last week I had a pretty young thing come in who would have been just right. The horrible thing about death is, it is always taking people and it never cares about their age.'

'Speaking of which...'

'Oh?'

'She needs to be of a certain age.' 'What do you mean?'

'Anything above twenty, for example. I don't want a young girl. I'm not a freak.'

#6

Cold Feet. No Pulse Either.

The rain lashed down heavily on the living room window of Robert's home forcing him to turn the television up a notch or two louder. He didn't know why he bothered. The mumbled dialogue coming from the film he was watching was laughable. The screenplay was clearly written by a child, or an imbecile. But that was what rainy Sundays was all about, watching crap films on the television which required little to no thought. He had only put it on in an effort to distract his mind from the conversation he had had with Tom the day before, in the cafe. Since the chat we had found himself walking around in a permanent state of arousal which was both painful, after a while, and frustrating. The thing is, it probably wouldn't have been so bad had it not been for the extra details Tom had gone into at the table. Instead of just saying that he would wait for a nice looker to come in before sending the text message, which would have been fine, he started going into further details about how he would make it nice for Robert. After all, it was his first time and he wanted to make it special for him. He said that he would light some of those scented candles you got from the majority of

greeting card shops, of all places, to take some of the strange smells from the room (mostly a mixture of clinical cleaning materials and death, a weird combination) and that he would also take in some pretty underwear. When he suggested the latter, Robert just looked at him with a bemused expression on his face. Tom explained that the bodies were usually naked and he didn't feel that was good enough for Robert. He carried on by explaining how it was good to see a woman who made an effort and wore sexy, matching underwear. Somehow, by staying covered with such skimpy lingerie, it made it seem that little bit more sexy than just seeing them lying there completely naked. Especially when - under the make-up, breast enhancing bras and various other tricks women used to appear better than they actually were - they could be a little... Different to how you imagined. Their tits would sag off to the side, their bushes could be slightly longer than you have imagined with - usually - one stray pubic hair that much longer than the rest, curling out at a weird angle and their vaginas themselves could have been different to the ones you see in porno movies too. For example, in the films, they tend to look neat and pretty. In reality they can sometimes look like a well-split axe wound or have a pair of unbelievable meat curtains hanging there which need opening up before a glimpse of inner cunt can be found. It didn't sound pretty the way Tom described it but - even so - it was enough to send a virgin's mind into overdrive, especially when the weather outside was lousy and there was nothing else to do.

Robert had run through the scenario in his head over and over again. He would open the door and step into the room. Considering it housed many dead people in various drawers dotted around the room, the room itself was warmer than he had imagined thanks to Tom putting out a small heater for him. The girl was not lying on a metal table, as expected, thanks to (again) Tom who had rested her on a black sheet. Black, instead of white, because the white sheet would mark too easily, Tom had explained. She did not have a sheet covering her, as Robert imagined most corpses would have thanks to seeing them presented in such a way in the movies he had seen. She was just lying there in black underwear. Silk panties and a matching bra. Her make-up had been applied nicely, Robert presumed another little touch by his friend, and she smelt of a sweet perfume. Before Robert did anything else, he set his mobile phone to the side of the room on loud so that if Tom called - warning him someone was coming - he didn't miss the ringing. The way he imagined the scenario playing through, the phone did not ring. Robert approached the table and unbuttoned the one button on his slacks. He undid his fly and pulled out his erection. Standing there, looking at the body lying before him, he started to stroke himself. After a couple of minutes teasing himself, he imagined pulling her knickers down and putting them in his pocket and he imagined standing there, looking at her bare cunt for a moment, taking it all in. It would be his first glimpse of female genitalia that hadn't been on a magazine page or on a screen and he would want to savour every moment of it, maybe even take a cheeky snapshot of it with his mobile phone just in case his memory ever struggled to recall the image. The scenario he painted often skipped the fumbling around, trying to slide his penis into the lubricated vagina. It also skipped out on the idea of foreplay but that wasn't because he was opposed to the idea of playing with her breasts, or even kissing around her pussy before pushing his tongue deep inside her. In actual fact, he quite liked the idea of doing those things. It was just - for now - he was more interested in the sensation of having his cock gripped by a real vagina. Some of the toys felt good, for sure, and some of them even promised a sensation close to the real thing but he wanted to know for sure. After all, these days, they put anything on packages these days to sell their products and it wouldn't have quite the same impact if the makers of, say, this vibrating pussy promised a feeling nothing like the real thing but, in its own right, nice enough... Christ, though, what would it feel like for real? Would it be tight? Would he feel ribbed textures inside as he slid in and out, like some of the toys, or tiny little bumps? Would it be warm? Wet? Cold? More to the point would he enjoy it after all these years of waiting? Maybe he had gotten so used to the feeling of various toys, or his Real Doll, that the real thing would be ruined for him now? He shook his head at the thought. It can't be. If toys were better, more people would be turning to them and less interested in wasting time - and in some cases money - chasing the real thing. Instead of conversations with his friends down the pub, discussing this notch on the bedpost or this dirty little slag or that whore or - maybe - this innocent little thing they had managed to corrupt and ruin, they'd be talking about which toy cunt they had fucked instead. Robert thought for a moment, as the naff film continued failing to distract him, and, after a moment, decided he was sure there had never been a conversation between him and his friends about fucking sex toys. Did they even give them a try when going through a dry patch? At a guess, he would say no. It was only him who stooped to those levels of self-pleasure.

Robert finally realized that the film wasn't helping him put the thoughts of what was soon to be happening from his mind and so switched channels, and continued to do so until he found something more of interest. In this instance, it was some documentary series following a police patrol unit in a town not so far from his own. It wasn't great television but he figured it might hold his attention more than the film he had been watching. Hopefully enough, at least, to be able to stop thinking about the possibilities of what Tom offered. On the off chance it didn't hold his attention, he kept the control close to hand.

*

Sunday came and went, wasted away in front of the television with only a quick conversation with the man who dropped off Robert's Chinese takeaway, later in the day. Monday was a typical day of working in the office, dealing with customers calling in with various complaints. No phone call from Tom though. Tuesday was also quiet and - later in the day - Robert found himself wondering whether this was going to happen at all. Had his friend taken his money and run off? If he had, could Robert tell anyone? Not exactly something he could go to the police for. He laughed at the prospect of having to explain the problem, playing through the scenario in his over-active mind.

'Right. So. You... You are saying you paid him £250 so you could...' The police would pause, unsure of how to finish the sentence. Perhaps even wondering if he *wanted* to finish it. Were people really this sick? Tom might get a ticking off from the police, true, but chances are Robert would be locked up in a mental home instead before he even had the opportunity to finish his sentence.

It was Wednesday afternoon when Robert picked up the phone and called through to Tom. The office staffroom was quiet with only Robert in it now. Everyone else had gone back to work from their lunch-break whereas he still had fifteen minutes left having purposefully started his lunch break a little later than his colleagues. He was sitting at a table with his back to the wall. With the phone pressed to his ear, he kept an eye on the door just in case someone came in - not that they had an obvious reason to. Nothing had been left on the tables that they could have claimed to have accidentally forgotten and the tea and coffee machine was out in the main foyer after management decided the small staffroom would get too crammed if it were kept where Robert was sitting now. Robert didn't believe their reasoning. He believed they just wanted to keep an easier eye on those who abused having access to free hot drinks. Some staff did, after all, take the piss with repeated trips to the machine when, truthfully, they should have been working. One unnamed staff member had been known to drink six coffees in the morning and more in the afternoon when the machine was hidden away in the staffroom. What frustrated the management more was not the fact he was wasting so much time avoiding work but the fact he never drank the whole drink! He'd make it, have half and then bin it later when he went to get a fresh cup. Now the machine was in the foyer, the breaks he took had been more than halved.

'Hello?' Tom finally answered the phone.

'It's me.'

'Caller ID. Wonderful thing. What's up, Rob?' 'I was just wondering if...'

'Nothing.' Tom knew what he was phoning for. He was actually surprised he hadn't heard from him sooner. 'Some young kid, a boy before you ask, was brought in. Poor bastard was hit by a car and pronounced D.O.A. Couple of oldies came in. There was a stabbing in our local a few days ago which came to its conclusion with the aggressor now facing a murder charge. Again, male victim. Only girl I had, who you'd have considered to be of age, was so fucked up from a fall that none of her limbs were facing the right way. Bent up like a fucking pretzel.'

'Right. Okay.'

'I told you when we met, you need to be patient.' 'I know I just...'

'Unless you aren't fussy in which case I am sure I'll have someone soon enough for you. The bent up girl has already gone off for her funeral so she is no good but the next time...'

'No, that's fine. I can wait. Just making sure you were still...'

'Trust me. I'm fine with this. Looking forward to helping a friend out.'

'Thank you.'

'No, thank *you*.' Tom didn't say it but he was grateful for Robert's inability to find himself a living, breathing lover. Thanks to him, he had at least one payment towards a bill. Play his cards right - and he planned to - and there was definitely the possibility for more cash. Tom continued, 'Look, I have to get ready for work. Quit panicking, this will happen. Okay?'

'Okay.'

'And when it does...' Tom laughed. 'You're in for a fucking treat.'

'Don't forget,' Robert said. 'Our secret.'

'I promise, you do as I say and you stick to our plan - no one will ever know. Okay? Besides, I have just as much to lose as you. For starters I would lose my job and if that were to happen I can kiss my career goodbye. You think people would want to employ me in this industry again if they found out what we were doing.'

'I guess.'

'Trust me, everything will be fine.' Tom finished by saying, 'Keep your phone on you, as we discussed, Death doesn't tend to be fussy about when He comes visiting. Soon as something comes in, I'll give you a bell. Cool?'

'All good.'

'Nice one. Chat soon.' And, with that, Tom hung his phone up. Robert stayed there a moment with the phone pressed to his ear. There was no hiding his obvious disappointment. He had been hoping Tom was going to answer the phone with the news someone had come in and he was welcome to go to the hospital tonight to visit them. But then, Robert perked up a little, just because no one was there now - it didn't mean they wouldn't be there later. As Tom had said, Death comes when Death chooses to come and not necessarily when it is convenient to people. Fingers crossed that somewhere, soon, a pretty girl would suddenly drop down dead. Preferably in a way which left her body looking good. Robert put his phone away, put the leftovers from his lunch in the bin and headed on back to work.

#7

Her name is Sheri. Her name was Sheri.

Sheri McDaniel wasn't just one of the prettiest girls in the waiting room, she was one of the prettiest girls in the whole town. Now in her mid- twenties, she had spent much of teenage years working as a model for a catalogue. She would be given clothes to wear, a photographer would snap her and then she would appear in the catalogue with each item of clothing clearly labeled with its name and price, along with an order number. It was good money and - better yet for Sheri - it was easy money. The modelling continued into her early twenties but progressed from catalogue shoots to more risqué shoots for lad's magazines which often required full-on nudity although, in fairness, it didn't mean you saw anything other than her nipples. For example, if she were fully naked, she would have a prop, or hand, in front of her private area to stop the photo from becoming full on pornographic. She had dirty blonde hair with brown eyes. She was a perfect size ten with curves in just the right places and - although they hid it well - she was often disliked by other girls because they were, to put it bluntly, jealous of her. She was a pretty girl with a good personality and she was making good money. Emphasis on the *was* making good money. At the age of twenty-two she met a new cameraman named Johnny. He was good looking and many people considered her well out of his league. Those same people were nothing if not surprised when he asked her out after a shoot and she agreed, especially as she wasn't short of offers - especially from footballers. She didn't like "celebrities" though. She found they came with baggage and were always on the lookout for someone, or something, better. She liked

Johnny because he was good enough looking, had a steady job and - more importantly to her - had a great personality. Unlike other men, he treated her like a Princess as opposed to some slut who gets her baps out for some trashy lads' mag. One date turned to two. Two dates turned to three, three to four and - within a month - they were going steady and calling each other "boyfriend" and "girlfriend". It was around this time, Sheri's life started to change, and not necessarily for the better.

First the possessiveness came. Sheri would want to go out with her friends, for a quiet night in one of the town's nicer bars, but Johnny wouldn't let her. If she went he would sulk like a petulant child and would proceed to text her all night asking what she was doing and making her feel guilty by complaining that he was bored. Nine times out of ten, when he did this, she would make excuses and go round to see him instead - pushing her friends to one side, much to their frustration (they could see exactly what he was doing). Second came the request - no, the demand - for her to stop working in the industry in which she was starting to create a name for herself. When asked why she should stop, Johnny said he didn't like the idea of loads of lads whacking themselves off to pictures of his partner. When she stated she didn't see what the problem was, he told her to look at it from his point of view. He asked her how she would feel if he were the one appearing in magazines and other girls were fucking themselves senseless with toys and fingers whilst imagining riding his cock. He painted a vivid picture for her and - of course - she didn't like it. Before the month was out she had turned down more job offers than she had accepted and within two months she was no longer taking any. Instead she was sitting in his apartment flicking through the job pages of the local paper looking for anything and everything to bring in some money. The more she looked, the more depressed she got though. She had left college with no A-Levels and - as a result - she was finding herself under-qualified for any of the jobs which would pay anything remotely close to what she had been getting as a model. Johnny told her to aim lower, start at the bottom and work her way up, but she didn't want to. And - another of his suggestions - she certainly didn't want to be earning minimum wage as a waitress in some shitty little diner somewhere... Soon after, the money problems started and the arguments became more frequent. The Honeymoon period was over - more so when she announced she was pregnant. His response being to unceremoniously dump her which is why she was now sitting in this waiting room. A waiting room not for benefits (something else she disagreed with), nor to do with her pregnancy. It was a waiting room for the next stage of the government run medical trials she had been accepted into - mainly thanks to her current condition.

'Miss McDaniel?' a doctor called into the waiting room from a small doorway opposite where Sheri was sitting. She put her hand up, acknowledging his call, and pulled herself up out of the seat. Six months pregnant now and she was getting bigger by the day and certainly more uncomfortable. With a hand on her aching back, she walked towards the doctor who smiled kindly at her. He held the door open for Sheri before closing it as she stepped into his modest sized office. The office itself was on the fourth floor of one of Southampton hospital's many wings. The whole wing was set up specifically for these various tests and were visited by people from all walks of life. Some volunteers were there for extra cash to see them through another holiday, or to pay off some debts or even just to treat a loved-one. To most people it was - without a shadow of a doubt - easy money and even if things didn't go smoothly (maybe they were allergic to what they were experimenting with) then they took comfort in the fact that the money was good. Especially for Sheri. Sheri was paid more due to her condition. A higher payout for higher risks - the worst risk being the very possible danger of something happening to the baby; a risk she deemed acceptable given the high-end four digit payout at the end of the month. Anyway, she didn't feel as though she had much of a choice. She was a single parent with no family around to help and she didn't want to be one of those single mums living on crappy benefits. She had never claimed money from the government (with regards to benefits offered) and didn't want to start now. Even though the cash was there to help people in real trouble, she didn't want to be a charity case. No way. This money, from this month long experiment trialling a new pill, would definitely be enough to tide her over for a while. Certainly enough to pay three months of rent and leave money left over for food each month, so long as she shopped carefully for the latter.

The doctor offered Sheri a seat and she gladly sat down again, despite having been seated for nearly thirty minutes out in the waiting room. She had no idea why she always got there early. He was always running late and she had lost count of the number of times she had thumbed the various publications in the waiting room: magazines which were already several months old. They were so old in fact that all crosswords, on the back pages, had been completed. Sheri recalled the first time she noticed they were filled in. She had wondered whether it was one person doing all the puzzles in one sitting as opposed to lots of people helping to finish them over various visits. Maybe, she had thought, the doctor had been running *really* late that day or, another possibility, the person responsible for completing the puzzles was some kind of genius.

'How is the rash?' the doctor asked as Sheri took her seat next to his cluttered table. The doctor immediately turned away from Sheri before she had the chance to answer. He positioned his fingers on his keyboard, ready to make notes when she started to speak. His unnecessarily direct question (nothing like cutting to the chase) was in reference to a rash which had developed on her chest after the last drug administration and - rightly so - had caused some concern amongst the staff who decided to keep her in for twenty four hours so they could monitor both her and her baby's vitals.

'I used a cream on it,' Sheri answered in a matter of fact tone, 'and it went pretty quickly.'

'That's good.'

'Or rather, most of it went. There are still some spots there but they don't itch, or anything. They're definitely going.'

'Good, good.' He quickly made some notes before asking a second question. For a second time, he didn't look at her as he asked, 'Any other symptoms?'

'Not that I am aware of. I saw the nurse earlier who went through my pulse, blood pressure and bits... She said everything was normal.'

'Good.' The doctor finished making notes and finally turned to Sheri. 'And in yourself you're feeling happy?'

'I'm still a little stressed by everything.' She didn't need to go into it with him. She always saw the same doctor and they had spoken of her position before, in one of the earlier consultations they had had together. She told him she was worried about raising a child on her own, she was stressed about money and how she didn't like where she was living at the moment; a small flat on a council estate. Her accommodation was given to her by the government when Johnny had kicked her to the curb. The only help she begrudgingly accepted having lost her old apartment. She couldn't afford her old place, having stopped the modelling, and - having turned so many jobs down - she couldn't get back *into* the modelling again to get herself out of the shit. She had become too unreliable to count on in the eyes of the publishers and photographers. When one did say they were thinking of employing her, someone else would put them off by asking if they remembered that time she didn't show up to one of her bookings and cancelled another. Needless to say, they soon changed their mind and employed someone else instead.

The doctor nodded. 'Any more problems with the neighbours?'

The flat was nice enough inside, considering it was a council property. The smell of death still lingered in the air though no matter how many cans of air freshener she used to try and disperse it. Previous owner had had a seizure after an overdose and dropped dead. It was a fortnight before they found him but that was by the by. The flat *was* nice enough inside, despite the smell, but the area outside was anything but nice. Youths hung around in the stairwells, smoking anything from weed to crack whilst discussing who to rob next, and the walls were painted in ugly graffiti that had been sprayed not by a talented individual expressing creative freedom but rather, a misfit bunch of idiotic thugs who just wanted to mark their territory. It was a shit-hole but what made it worse was that people around the estate knew her. Not everyone but lads of a certain age. Lads who had seen the pictures in various magazines and no doubt masturbated over them too. Not a day went by when these lads didn't ask her if she'd want to fuck them. They offered drugs, money and even a "real cock" in exchange. Each time, she politely declined which soon made them turn on her. Instead of the propositions she soon became the victim of being spat on (they believed she considered herself "too good" for them) and name-calling. On one occasion someone threw a rock through her window and - on more than one occasion - they would post used condoms through the letterbox. She didn't go to the police like the doctor suggested. He had told her that, with the condoms as evidence, the culprit - or culprits - would be found soon enough, if they had a record already that was. She declined his advice. In this estate, you don't go to the police. You don't want people thinking you're a grass. Not in this estate. Sheri told the doctor, 'They've been quiet enough recently. I think they're bored.'

'That's good.'

And there was silver lining in the dark cloud too. 'At the end of the month, payment should come too which will be enough of a deposit to move out.'

'That's good.' A staple answer for everything. 'Where would you move too?'

'Not sure. Nowhere too expensive. It won't be the best place but it will be better than where I am now.'

'Of course.' The doctor smiled. He pushed himself away from the table and stood up. He asked, 'Are you ready for today's dosage then?' Sheri nodded and also stood. 'We'll be upping it a little today so they will most likely request you stay in so they can monitor you again. Did you bring your overnight bag?'

'Yes I did.'

'Excellent. Well then...' He walked to the door and continued, 'If you want to head on down, the nurses will get you all settled and start the dosage. I have a few more people to see here but I will come on down and see you later: check that everything is okay.'

Sheri smiled and thanked the doctor as she stepped from his office. That was the last time the doctor would see her alive. Within the next two hours, she would have a total shut down of her internal organs, despite their best efforts to keep them going. Bad news for Sheri, the baby and the medical trial but great news for...

*

'Robert!' Tom was standing in the morgue with his phone pressed to his ear. On the bench before him, covered by a thin white sheet, was the body of a once-famous glamour model. 'You need to get down here!' Tom said when the person on the other end of the phone acknowledged himself to be

Robert. On the other end of the line, Robert said he would be there soon and then hung up. Tom put his phone down on one of the many metal side tables, lining the walls, and turned his attention to the girl. It was midnight. Robert was at home and could be here within thirty minutes. Tom had a lot of work to do to make her look pretty for him.

He removed the sheet and gazed upon her body. For a split second he contemplated leaving the gown on her as it helped cover the baby bump but there was no denying it was a bit of a mood killer. Especially given the fact some vomit had stained around the neck line from where it erupted from her mouth during one of the many convulsions she had suffered before death. He shook his head. It was no good, the gown had to go.

#8

Pretty.

The gown was folded and put into the very same carrier bag Tom had brought the underwear in. The gown stank of the recently dead and he wanted to bin it but he knew - when Robert was done - he might need to put the girl back in it. Tom turned back to the dead girl. She was wearing the lingerie he had brought in for her, stolen from his wife on the day Robert agreed to the deal. Or rather, she was wearing *some* of the lingerie Tom had stolen for her. The hold-up stockings were in the carrier bag, ready to be taken home again and disposed of. Damned things split when he tried to get them over her feet up and her legs. One split at the toes and the other split up the seams. Not sexy or romantic when they're ripped to fuck and so they had to go. Tom had cursed himself for being a clumsy idiot. Now though, as he looked at the girl, he wasn't swearing at himself. She was looking sexy. Tom laughed to himself, *dead* sexy. If this was going to be a business, there was the name he would use.

Hanging on a metal hook behind the door was Tom's coat. He walked over to it and removed a small bottle of perfume he had purchased for the occasion. He hadn't stolen it from his wife as she was precious about her scents and would definitely miss it, but it was the same brand. Keeping the smell the same kept things simple for himself as it meant he didn't go home smelling of another woman. Not that it mattered given how things were going at home. Who he slept with was none of her business anymore but... He didn't want to have to explain himself, or tell her to mind her own business. He couldn't be bothered with the argument. Simpler life and all that. He walked back over to the body and sprayed the corpse both directly and around her. The sickly sweet scent of the perfume clung to her skin and hung in the air. Another thought popped into Tom's head and - for a second time - he couldn't help but to giggle. The thought? This dead woman was as cold as his living, breathing woman back home. If anything, there was more love in the corpse. Another laugh. The love will be spilling out of her in an hour, or so. He shuddered at the thought, not of semen dribbling from a vagina but of semen dribbling from a *dead* vagina. He tried to shake the thought from his head. Now is not the time to start being judgemental, especially if he wants Robert to keep funding him. He needs Robert to think this is perfectly normal and - more than that - actually fun too.

The girl was ready now. She was as good as she was going to get. She smelled slightly better, thanks to the perfume, and she looked a little better thanks to the sexy underwear Tom had taken for her. Underwear that Tom knew Sally wouldn't miss, unless she was planning on fucking another stranger that is. Tom cast a look around the room and remembered something else he had brought for the occasion. Scented candles, another mask for the room's true stink. The candles, like the bra and knickers, were stolen from the house. Knowing time was against him, he hurried to the far side of the room and opened the carry case he used for his laptop. Tucked inside the flap, in a zipped compartment, was a handful of "taster" candles his wife had received one Christmas. They had the same scent as the proper candle but were much, much smaller and stood up of their own accord without the need of a candlestick holder. Lighting them as he went, he dotted them around the room. Immediately he realised his rookie error in that all the smells were different. It would have been better had they been the same. He shrugged. *Fuck it*. A weird mix of different flavours would still be better than the smell of the dead, a strange musty scent reminiscent of old people, mould and urine. Ah the smell of the dead, a definite potential passion killer. The smell of the dead, soon to be all but gone thanks to the fact all candles were now lit and slowly burning away. Tom already had the excuse ready if someone did come barging in unannounced. He would simply tell them it was for his benefit having grown tired of the smell of bodies. No one could argue with that although hospital management could tell him to get rid of them as they were a definite fire risk. Tom had already thought about that though and knew the chances of anyone coming down from that particular department were slim to none. They never visited as Tom's department, and job, were a necessity. Cuts could be made throughout the hospital - much to the frustration of the staff - but everyone knew death never stopped no matter how hard people fought. The mortuary was definitely an unpleasant necessity.

From across the room, where he had left it after calling Robert, Tom's mobile phone started to vibrate across the cold, metal surface of the worktop. From where he was standing, Tom could see Robert's contact photo flashing up on screen with each vibration. This is it. Showtime. Tom reached for the phone and answered it as he pressed it to his ear. 'Hi.'

'It's me.' Robert sounded nervous down the other end of the line, a quiver in his voice. 'I'm here.' He quickly added, 'As in, I'm in the hospital now. Should I just come on down?'

'Sure. I'm just finishing up. Do you know the way?'

'There are signs.'

'You won't have access to the mortuary itself. Need a code for the door and they would probably ask questions if they saw you inputting it. When you get to the set of double doors with electronic keypad, give me a missed call and I will come and get you.' He added, 'Oh and look sad. That way if anyone sees you, they'll think you've just lost someone close to you.'

'Okay.'

'Hope you're excited, buddy, she is a looker!' Tom was well aware of how nervous Robert sounded. He didn't want him to be nervous. He wanted him to be excited! He was about to have sex after all! The more he enjoyed it, the more chance he would want to come back and Tom could earn himself more money. Tom didn't wait for an answer from Robert. He hung the phone up and put it on the side from where he'd originally taken it. A quick look around the room and it was obvious it was as good as it was going to get. The girl looked good too. Well, as good as a dead chick could look. Tom had used his hands to "comb" her hair as best as he could and she smelled more acceptable than having just been left without a spray of perfume. Although... Tom realised he hadn't paid much attention to the downstairs area. An area so new to Robert that it could very well come under close scrutiny and - with that in mind... Nothing worse than a stinky pussy. Tom approached the body and pulled the knickers to one side. Another good thing the girl had going for her was the state of her vagina. It looked as though it must have been worked on at some time, from some kind of designer vagina doctor. Damned thing was immaculate with its slim pink lips and perfect slit. Tom didn't have to get any closer to realise the scent wasn't up to much though. Hardly surprising. During her seizure, she must have pissed herself - a not uncommon situation for "fitting" people to find themselves in. Just another thing to cause them a little embarrassment when they stopped fitting, so long as they haven't died that is. Never fear, though. Tom had the perfect thing.

Hurrying over to his carry-case, the same one he had got the candles from, he reached in and removed a small tube of lubricant. Again - this too had been taken from his house. Purchased months, and months, ago when he was trying to convince his then-loving wife to let him try anal. Despite the promise of being gentle, it was a non-starter and the tube had never been opened. Until now that is. Walking back over to the corpse, Tom broke the seal and squeezed some of the clear gel onto his fingers. He pulled them close to his nose and breathed in deeply. The packet didn't lie, it did smell just like strawberries. He dabbed a little from fingertip to tongue. Tasted like them too. He set the tube down next to the body on the off-chance Robert wanted some more and he wiped the little he had squeezed onto his fingers down on the dead woman's pussy, ensuring that he got the slit wet. At least this way, he thought, it would make the initial penetration easier and, if Robert fancied a taste, give the vagina a more fruity and pleasant taste. Wiping his fingers on his trousers, Tom leaned down to the gash and breathed in. Death's aroma wasn't as bad now it had been mixed with strawberry. Again, it wasn't perfect but it was the best that he could offer. He stood up straight and looked at her body. All things considered, she was pretty. He smiled to himself, she would do.

*

Robert walked down the final corridor he was permitted to go down. At the far end of it was a set of double doors and he could already see the numeral keypad to the side, attached to the wall. Above the door was a sign which read "Mortuary". By now Robert's heart felt as though it were in the back of his throat; an uncomfortable feeling and one he believed would be there to stay, at least until he got back to the safety of his home. Home. A little voice in the back of his head suggested he would be better off turning right around and heading home now. A little whisper, *Just go home*. Despite the voice, he reached into his phone and miss-called his friend signalling that he was there waiting for him. Hanging up, he put the phone back in his pocket and waited, nervously, with his back to the wall. He told himself, and the little voice still nagging him to run away, that he didn't have to go through with anything. He could just go in, see the woman lined up for him, thank Tom and then go home. No one was going to actively force him to do anything. He was still arguing with himself when the door suddenly opened. Tom was standing there with a smile on his face. He didn't look nervous at all, which surprised Robert. Sure, Tom wasn't about to have sex with a dead person but he still had a reason to be nervous. If something happened, if they were caught... It was still his job, his career, on the line. Possibly even his freedom too. Necrophilia might be a grey area but Robert was pretty sure pimping was illegal.

'Alright?' Tom extended his hand. Robert shook it. That little voice in his head pointing out that this had been the first time the two of them had ever shaken hands. Tonight, they were not friends, they were business partners. 'Come on through.' He held the door open as Robert stepped through. Tom released the door and it banged shut and locked behind him. 'This way.' Tom walked round Robert and led him through to where his evening's date was waiting for him. 'Remember to have your phone on loud. I'll be close-by outside keeping watch. Any issues, you can call me and I will come in. If anyone heads down, I will call you and you need to make sure everything is presentable for strangers to see, okay? Basically, just cover her up with a white sheet that's in a carrier bag on the side. Can't miss it.' He explained, 'There are candles in the room too but you can leave those. If anyone asks about them, that's down to me. I already have an excuse for having them there.' Tom turned into a room, pushing the door open as he did so. The morgue. Or, for the next hour anyway, the whore's bedroom. Robert didn't come in: he stopped in the doorway, visibly shaking. 'You okay there?' Tom asked. He could see the opportunity to earn extra money slowly slip from his fingers. Robert didn't answer him. He was just standing there with his eyes fixed on the dead body lying there in the black lingerie. 'Robert?' Tom tried to get his attention. 'Rob?!'

'Huh?' Robert turned to Tom.

'Hi. Welcome back. You okay?'

'Yes.'

'You going to come in or just stand there?'

'Sorry.' Robert stepped into the room but didn't go much further from the doorway. The door closed behind him. Robert's eyes were fixed back to the body. 'What was her name?'

'Sheri McDaniel. You recognise her? She was a glamour model a few years back. Every other week she would be in the lads' magazines and then - suddenly - she just vanished. No idea what happened there. Must have got bored doing it. Certainly didn't stop because of her looks. She is stunning. Even in death.'

'She pregnant?' Robert was staring at the bump.

'Not anymore but she was. Isn't a problem though. Doesn't mean you can't do what you want to do to her.

'No but…'

'And you never said anything about not wanting pregnant women.'

'No but I just didn't think…'

Tom interrupted him again and said, 'You said no one underage. She isn't underage and - come on - look at her. She is stunning. Trust me, this is as good as it is probably going to get. And her pussy. Man, you should see her snatch. It's a piece of fucking art, mate.' Tom noticed a small smile on Robert's face. He was winning him round slowly but surely. He cut to the chase and asked, 'What are you thinking?'

'How did she die?'

'She was taking part in a medical trial the hospital was running. Something went wrong. Not sure what yet. They called me up just as my shift started. They want an autopsy done by morning to try and figure out what the Hell happened and how they can stop it happening again.'

'A medical trial?'

Tom shrugged. 'Don't ask me, mate. I don't get involved with those. Random tests on willing volunteers on new medications. Not often they die, though. Sure you get people have adverse reactions from time to time but not normally death. Still she knew the risks and her loss is your gain.' He asked, 'You like her?'

'She is pretty.'

'She is stunning, not just pretty. And - just think - a girl like this... None of us would have got a look in when she was alive. None of us. Not even God's gift to women Jason.' Tom laughed. 'I reckon, if I call him, he'd come down here and have a crack too.' That was it. That was all Tom had to say. If the girl was good enough for Jason, the most successful "puller" of the group, then she was definitely good for Robert.

'And I get an hour from when I start or from when we walked in the room?'

'From the moment I close the door. Like I said, just keep the phone close-by just in case.'

'Of course.'

'So want me to leave you two to get better acquainted?' Tom asked. There was a long enough pause to make him worry that Robert was going to cancel. A long enough pause to make him glad he had told him there were no refunds on the money already paid. The money, already spent. Little did Tom realise, Robert was still having an internal argument with himself: one side of him wanted to leave and the other side wanted to stay.

'Yes please,' he finally said to Tom with his eyes still fixed on the girl. More specifically he was looking at the gusset area of her knickers, wondering what was beneath. Or rather what *it* looked like under there. Tom smiled and nodded. Without another word he stepped from the room, closing the door behind him. 'Just you and me then,' Robert said quietly. He glanced up to the clock on the wall. His hour had started.

#9

True Love.

Robert approached the table in the centre of the room. The heavy, hard beating of his heart reminding him of the main difference between him and his date for the night. He was alive and she was dead. He felt awkward standing there, before her. Was he supposed to introduce himself? Was he supposed to say something else? Or was he supposed to just whip it out and get involved? No talking, no romance, just stick it in and fuck away. This wasn't how he pictured his first time: neither his first date nor his first time having intercourse. He was supposed to meet his lady at a restaurant and not just any restaurant at that but the finest in town: a small Italian place called Keats, just on the outskirts of Romsey. He would have taken her a small bouquet of flowers purchased from a florist as opposed to a petrol station. He would greet her with a kiss to the cheek and the waiter would offer to take their coats and put the flowers in water to save them from spoiling before they left. When they approached the table, Robert would take the job of the waiter showing them to their place, and he would pull her chair from underneath her table, offering her to sit. She would sit and make herself comfortable as he'd take his own place, opposite her. The waiter would hand them a menu each and offer them their first drink of the evening. Robert would ask whether his date wanted a bottle of wine to share and, if so, whether she preferred red, or white. She would start with water and suggest they order the wine later, when they knew the dishes they'd be eating. Conversation would flow freely and easily. They would listen, laugh and love as they shared stories or life, love lost and hopes for the future. A first date with so much in common. A first date which would lead on to several more equally great dates before they'd share their first, perfect kiss.

Robert would be nervous when it came down to the kiss. His date would be too. So much rested on the first kiss as it told them both if there was any real chemistry there. Sometimes you can kiss someone and it just feels all wrong. It's wet and sloppy or you feel as though you're kissing a family member. You realise the person standing before you is more friend than girlfriend or boyfriend. They had nothing to be nervous about though. The kiss would be perfect and bolts of electricity would tingle in their bodies, just beneath the skin. Tingles of pleasure as they shared the first of many passionate embraces with the moon illuminating the evening sky, high up in the air larger than it has ever appeared before. A light rain cooling their increasing temperature. Robert would pull away smiling. She'd be standing there a moment with her eyes closed a split second longer and her lips pursed together, lost in the moment. She'd open her eyes and smile, embarrassed that Robert was looking at her with such a burning intensity in his eyes. He would suggest a walk. A nice walk to cool them both off. A little walk through the local park, hand in hand. The rain didn't matter, they were both already wet (her in more ways than one) and it meant they got to continue this particular date a while longer. More laughter, more stories and - standing by the lake's river lined with trees - another romantic kiss. This is his woman and this was her man. The search would be over. They would have found one another and soon enough the relationship would be cemented by taking it to the next stage on. She would stay the night with him.

He wouldn't want her to come and stay at his house. He is not embarrassed by it and she would have seen it on numerous occasions, even asking him for a guided tour at some point. For their first night together, though, he wanted to treat her to a hotel. There was a nice five star establishment in Burley: a large building hidden within the New Forest. Robert had seen it on many an occasion but never had the opportunity to stay. The long weekend he planned was both a treat for him and a treat for her. It would have been something they would have both remembered for all the right reasons. The night would start with quickly unpacking in the suite he would have booked. Next, they would have had a nice meal in the fine restaurant within the hotel. With dinner, there would have been consumption of wine which would have helped to relax them both. Throughout the meal, they would have flirted easily with one another and both would have felt the excitement build towards what was to come. Speaking of which...

Upstairs, in the room, she would go to the bathroom to freshen up. He would wait on the settee. Waiting on the bed seemed too forward and he didn't want her to feel any pressure as to what he expected. He would be happy to just spend time with her. If nothing happened but cuddling, he would have been fine with that. If something happened, obviously he would have been fine with that too. But it had to be her decision. The bathroom door would open and she would come out. With what she would be wearing, her decision would be obvious. She would ask him, teasingly, how she looked. He would try and answer but would stumble over the words; words which were meant to say how amazing she looked. She would be wearing stockings with suspenders, along with a silk negligee. Whilst in the bathroom, she would have re-applied her make-up - not that she needed any to look beautiful to him - and she would have messed her hair slightly. The shy girl he had met on the first date would be gone and standing before him would be a woman who knew what she wanted and how to to get it. He would smile as he approached her. They would embrace in a passionate kiss and - when they pulled away - she would push him back onto the bed, moaning that he was wearing too many clothes. She would lean down and pulls his trousers down, and off. She would toss them to the side of the room. He would sit up and remove his own socks before she'd push him back again and pull his shorts down, freeing his erection - the sight of which does not disappoint after the build-up and anticipation. This was how Robert imagined it. Years of being alone gave him plenty of time to really get the scenario built-up in his mind, refining it until it was a perfect start to a perfect relationship. How he imagined it was much, much different to what he was now presented with.

*

Sheri didn't introduce herself. Neither did she say she was happy to see Robert or thank him for coming. But then, he didn't have any flowers for her either. He figured, within the next week or so, she would be the recipient of numerous flowers and wreaths anyway. She didn't need more. Robert didn't say 'hello' to her either. He stood there, nervously shifting his weight from one foot to the other. He was conscious of the fact his friend was standing just the other side of the door and wondered whether he was listening, trying to hear how Robert was getting on. He tried to put the thought from his mind. Keep thinking that, he'd never be able to go through with this - that was, if he decided he *could* go through with it. Standing there, looking at this body, he wasn't able to see her as anything but a person. How did the judge think of her as anything else? More to the point - had the judge been in this position now, would he have been able to go through with it? Would he have been able to fuck her? Robert mentally berated himself, *This cost £250. Stop thinking about the damned judge.*

Nervously, he approached the table and - with a shaking hand - he reached out and touched her bare skin. Her leg. She was cold to the touch but he didn't pull his hand away.

'I'm sorry for what happened to you,' he said. He gently slid his hand up her leg to the bump in her belly. 'I'm sorry for what happened to both of you.' He looked at her face. She really was beautiful, even in death.

He touched the side of her face and gently
pushed a stray strand of hair back, tucking it
behind her ear. *Perfect*. Part of him wished
he had met her when she had a pulse. The
other part of him, the realist, reminded him
that it would never have happened. This girl
was way out of his league and the only way
he could have gotten this close was if she...
Well... The only way he could have gotten
this close was if she signed up for a medical
trial and died as a result of it. He leaned
down and tenderly kissed her on the
forehead. Cold and clammy but he could
imagine the warmth that used to be there.
He pulled away slightly and gazed upon her
face. He half expected her to be looking at
him with eyes open as opposed to closed.
But no, they were still shut. He leaned down
again and hovered with his face close to her
face. His lips inches from her lips. He kept
his eyes open, watching her own eyes.
When she didn't move, he gently gave her a
kiss on her lips. Dry and cracked. When she
failed to move again, he started to relax a
little. It was almost as though his fears were

born from believing this to be nothing more than a prank. He would start to get close and she would suddenly sit up and scream at him. Tom, meanwhile, would fly into the room with a camera in hand, laughing at Robert's panicked expression. This wasn't a prank. She was definitely dead.

Robert gently opened her mouth by pulling down on her chin. He ran his fingers along the inside of her lips. The inside was still a little wet. He guessed, as time went on, that too would dry out as the mouth stopped producing saliva. He leaned down again and kissed her open mouth. He didn't pull away. He closed his eyes and kissed her again. His tongue entered her mouth and explored for a moment or two before he pulled away and gagged violently. When she had died, or rather just before she had died, she must have thrown up. The lingering acidic, bitter taste of stomach bile lingered in her mouth. *Don't do that again*. He should have known better than to try and kiss her. When chatting with Tom, it was never about kissing. It was about losing his virginity. Once his stomach had settled, Robert turned back to her and pushed her chin up, closing her mouth back up. He wouldn't try kissing her again. Not there at least.

He run his hand down from the top of her breast to the bottom, cupping it through the bra. A gentle squeeze as his cock started to stiffen slowly. With his other hand, he took a hold of the bra and pulled it down on one side, exposing her bare breast. Her nipple was hard and perfectly formed. He looked at it for a moment before curiosity finally got the better of him and he leaned down to that too, and put it in his mouth. He sucked on it harder than would have been comfortable for a living, pregnant woman. His clear inexperience obvious as his tongue flicked against the nipple, hard and fast with no particular method. As he continued sucking, enjoying his *taste* of his first real breast, his hand moved over the bump in her belly down to her panties. For a moment they rested upon them with his palm against her pubic mound and his fingers curled around her undercarriage so that the tips rested against the gusset of the knickers. Erection not only hard now but straining against his shorts and trousers. With his other hand, he fumbled with his flies before undoing them. He reached into his trousers and started stroking himself, occasionally squeezing and teasing the shaft of his cock when he needed to slow his strokes down or risk ejaculating. In his head the girl was no longer a corpse but she was a person still and not an inanimate object. She wasn't dead either. She was alive. She was a willing participant, offering to lie motionless so that Robert could explore her body. In his head. He pulled away from her breast and looked at her face once more, sure that she would be looking down at him, smiling and with lust in her eyes. Nope. She hadn't moved. Still lying with closed eyes.

Robert was full of lust now. The thought of fucking her had taken a grip of his inexperienced body. He was breathing hard and fast. He sighed lustfully, 'You're so beautiful. Thank you for this.' He was so aroused that he didn't realise what he was saying, either that or he didn't care. *Thank you for this?* Thank her for what exactly? Dying? Robert moved back to the one exposed breast and started sucking for a second time as his fingers applied a little pressure to the gusset area of her knickers. He knew it wouldn't be long before he *had* to remove her underwear and see (and feel) what a real pussy was like. Slowly it started to dawn on him that he wanted more than an hour. He should have paid for longer. A thought popped in his head, *Can always come back.*

#10
Losing the cherry.

Black underwear on the floor in a messy heap. A sticky residue on the inside of the gusset which had turned Robert on more so. The illusion of wetness no doubt caused from where he'd been sucking on her tit. The reality being nothing more than it being some residue lube staining the material from when Robert had pushed it against her vagina. He didn't care for the truth and hadn't even put two and two together as he carefully parted her legs. One leg stayed on the table and the other swung down to the side of it. Her bare cunt was exposed for him to admire. For him to lust after. He stroked it with one finger at first, running the length of her wet slit (good old lube hiding the fact she was drier than the Sahara). He awkwardly pushed passed the perfect lips, forcing his finger deeper into the orifice. No romance. No foreplay. This was a man exploring for the first time, keen to feel the real thing. Some of the cheaper toys felt much different to this, and not in a good way. The expensive toys though, like the Real Doll and the Flesh-Lights - credit where it was due, they were fairly close. He pushed a second finger in before he slowly started to pump in and out, in and out, in and out - each thrust of his finger pushing the lube a little further inside of her making the cunt seem wetter. He wanted to be inside her. He wanted to feel the pussy around his dick. He wanted to know what it felt like yet he was worried that when he did push inside her, it would be over too soon. With his other hand still on his cock, stroking gently, he could feel the tip was wet with pre-cum. It wouldn't take much to push him over the edge. He removed his fingers and sniffed them, curious to know the smell of a real pussy. Strawberries. Not what he had expected despite the tube of lubricant being there, in plain sight, for him to see. He moved his head closer to her vagina and gave it a sniff. Definitely strawberries. Still stroking himself (gently) he gave it a slow, lingering kiss. Just a peck. When he licked his lips and got the taste of strawberries again, he dived deeper pushing his tongue up inside her, where his fingers had previously explored. Strawberries and a hint of something else. What was what? Chicken? He pushed his face up against the cunt as much as he could in an effort to get his tongue deeper inside of her. The other leg slipped from the table too. Both legs dangled either side as Robert climbed on trying to get deeper and deeper into her fruity vagina. Fruit and? Not chicken. He has definitely tasted it before though, or something similar at least. Memories were stirring but he couldn't place them. He wasn't put off or disgusted, though. It was nice. Far better than when he had practised on one of the many fake vaginas he had tried over the years; a little lick in an effort to learn how best to do it when faced with a real one like now. He licked up and around, circling motions inside her. What the Hell is....? He pulled out. Tuna. Strawberries and tuna, a strange mixture and yet.... He pushed his tongue inside her for a second time. A strange mixture and yet one that somehow worked.

Robert couldn't resist any further. He moved up the table so that his face was adjacent to hers. His chest pressed against her breasts. His belly squashed against her little bump. His cock nudging towards her ready vagina. A fleeting thought wondering how people fucked pregnant women when their bump was any bigger than this. As quickly as the thought came, it went and - with a bit of fumbling and a sigh - he pushed up inside her.

*

Robert's first time would have been in the hotel. The girl would have been wearing a black negligee with stockings and suspenders. She would push him back on the bed and help him remove her clothes.

She would then clamber on top of him and kiss him passionately as his hands explored her body, ending on her buttocks which he'd gently squeeze. They'd kiss for a while before he would flip her onto her back. He would now be on top of her. He would be kissing her, his hands still on her buttocks. Her hands would be on his arse too. They wouldn't be talking. The silence would be filled with the sounds of heavy breathing and lustful panting. She might, after more kissing, tell him that she wants to feel him inside her. She can't wait any longer. Robert would get up long enough to grab a rubber from the bedside cabinet next to the bed. A quick fumble with the silver foil wrapper and another fumble trying to roll the rubber sheath down the length of his shaft. She'd watch him doing it, slowly stroking herself as she did. Not because she needed to be more turned on but because it felt nice and she enjoyed watching him inadvertently play with himself. He'd smile at her when he was covered. She'd playfully motion for him to come back over to her, which he would. They'd kiss some more and she'd take his erection in hand and guide it into her. She'd gasp as it slid inside her, as would he. The build-up and anticipation for this very moment was worth it. It would feel amazing for the both of them. It would have been different to what Robert was experiencing now.

*

Robert let out a very audible sigh as his cock slid inside the girl. It felt good. There was a tightness which gripped him nicely. This was how he imagined it would feel. The only difference to the scenario painted in his head was the lack of sigh from the girl. Whilst his hands were on her body, her hands laid by her side, unmoving. He frowned, conflicted as to the thoughts going through his head. On the one hand it felt amazing and yet - on the other hand - it would have been better had she moved, had she sighed, had she touched him as he touched her. He pulled out slightly and then pushed back in. Another sigh. More confusion. The longer he stayed inside her, without her moving, the more he realised this wasn't right. It couldn't be further from "right". And, yet, he couldn't stop as it felt good, maybe better because it was so wrong. He closed his eyes to the reality of the situation and went back to imagining that she was alive, just lying still for him so he could do as he pleased and explore her as he saw fit. He started increasing the rhythm with which he thrust into her. There was no denying it felt good, no matter how wrong it felt. Just get it done. Just this once. Get it done and don't worry about the rights or wrongs. Enjoy it. Go with it. Let the orgasm build. Let it build and build. Feel the tingling. Robert stopped moving suddenly. His eyes wide. Her cunt had tightened to a vice-like grip.

'What the?' It continued getting tighter. Robert tried to pull out but couldn't. He was stuck fast. Panicked, he tried to pull out again but his dick was squeezed harder still to the point of bordering on painful. He reached down, the idea being to prise her pussy open with his hands. He frowned as he realised her pussy lips hadn't actually moved much, other than maybe gaping a little. They certainly hadn't tightened to the point of cutting off the blood circulation. He looked back to the door and went to call out to Tom but stopped at the last minute. He couldn't let Tom see him like this, stuck inside a dead woman. A predicament so fucked-up and unusual that he feared the situation would no longer be *their* secret and that Tom would tell everyone. *Hey, remember the time you got your dick stuck in a dead chick?*

Robert looked back at the corpse. Panic had well and truly set in as he tugged back again, hoping to suddenly pop out. Thoughts running through his head wondering as to whether this was because she was dead? Maybe some kind of internal tightening of the muscles? Maybe Rigor Mortis? *What the fuck was going on?* He reached down and slid a finger inside the pussy, squeezing it in along from the base of his shaft, and he pushed up until... Robert's eyes went wide. He screamed out, not in pleasure or pain but fear. Pure fear. Around his cock, squeezing him tightly, was a small hand. He removed his finger and pressed both hands down against the cold

metal table. He pushed down onto it with all of his weight in the hope he could slide himself from the dead woman's unwelcoming orifice. He didn't move though. He screamed again. Where was Tom? Why wasn't he running in to see what the screaming was about? Were the walls sound-proofed? They could have been. The amount of noisy equipment used within this room to cut up the dead... It made sense the room was sound-proofed. Even so, Robert called out, 'Tom! Help me! What the fuck! She's giving birth! TOM!' Still his friend did not come.

Robert felt something bump against his stomach. He lifted his weight off Sheri's dead body and looked down to her own stomach. Underneath his skin he could see a small imprint of a hand pushing through. He screamed again and watched in horror as the fingers spread out before curling inwards to a claw-like posture. Sheri's stomach skin pinched together as the hand closed around the other side of it. Robert struggled again to get himself free when - without warning - the corpse's stomach ripped open. Robert screamed and this time, he didn't stop as he watched the small head of a tiny baby push through the ripped-open stomach hole. Its eyes were clouded in Death's misted shroud. It's skin, pale beneath the layers of gore, covered in tiny blue and purple veins bulging from underneath. It wasn't

crying like some newborn babies. It was moaning, like one of the fictional undead seen in so many horror films before.

'This isn't happening! This isn't happening!' Robert screamed out loud. But it was happening. Pain from his cock being crushed in the unfeasibly strong grip, and fear from what he was seeing, mixed with thoughts asking how this could be happening crowded his mind. The only possible answer being that it was something to do with the medical trial. Some kind of adverse reaction to whatever had killed Sheri; a toxic concoction which had somehow brought some kind of life to the unborn child. Life and strength. Was it an accident? Was it planned? Was this the trial's end goal? Robert couldn't take his eyes from the dead baby's face as it tried to bite at his own stomach - just out of reach thanks to the umbilical cord tied tightly around its neck. Another thought rushed through his panicking, petrified mind: *If it could bring life to the unborn baby - life and strength - what about Sheri?* He looked up and screamed louder than before. Her eyes were fixed to his eyes. Her lips curled up with a low moan strained from her vocal cords. She craned her head up closer to Robert's and bit into his face. Her upper teeth tore through his nose as her bottom row of teeth ripped through his lower lip. As her jaw closed, the flesh between the two rows of teeth was mashed to an unrecognisable pulp. He couldn't scream anymore as blood poured from the fresh wound and Sheri continued to bite and tear and rip and shred at his face with her hands now pulling him down on top of her. With mum's help keeping Robert in place and close to her body, the baby was now able to get to Robert's stomach. As its tiny hand started clawing through Robert's stomach skin, muscle and then lining, Robert was perfectly still. Consciousness had been taken from him swiftly which was - for him - a blessing in disguise. Especially when the other tiny hand finally pulled Robert's now flaccid cock away from his spasming body.

*

It had been a little over an hour and all had been quiet in the main corridor. Tom had been surfing the Internet on his mobile phone, using the 4G signal as opposed to the hospital's weak WiFi. Given how quiet it was tonight, he didn't feel the need to disturb Robert. By giving him longer, he figured he would be more inclined to come back another time - should another pretty girl find herself in the mortuary. *Should* another pretty girl find herself there? That should have been *when*: when another pretty girl finds herself in the mortuary. Tom knew better than anyone that Death didn't care if you were young or old. When your time was up, your time was up. What he didn't know, though, was that thanks to some (nearly) successful medical trials - now when you died you didn't necessarily stay dead. You could come back. Kind of. Hence the "nearly". A little tweaking to the formula was needed to bring you back to life properly but the scientists had definitely made a positive start. They could reanimate a dead person and - in time - they were sure they could tame them to be how they were when they were alive the first time round. Just a few more medical trials were needed first, not that Tom would be around for them.

Tom slid the phone back in his pocket and walked over to the electronic keypad by the doorway. He keyed in the code and stepped through the door. He whistled as he walked down the corridor and wondered whether Robert was finished yet, or whether he had even started. Maybe he had spent the whole time just sitting with her, talking through his feelings? Tom chuckled at the thought and pushed the final door open. He stepped into the room and stopped dead. His eyes widened in horror. On the floor, by the table, was what remained of Robert's fucked up body. Half of his face was missing with only his tongue flapping around in the air as though he were trying to say something. His stomach ripped open with entrails splattered around him and his body twitching as though he were still trying to get up despite the horrific injuries. Sitting up, on the table,

Sheri was cradling her baby. The baby had not come from the vagina but seemed to have crawled out via the hole in *her* stomach. It wasn't screaming but moaning, as was she. As was Robert. *What the fuck*?

Tom screamed.

L - #0165 - 110723 - C0 - 175/108/8 - PB - DID3627097